aviatic

I met Ruby when we were both teenagers and homeless. Our stories are the same. We were both taken away from our families.
Ruby and I were together for thirty-eight years. We had two children and raised others as our own. Because we were taken away, family means everything. Through the years, Aboriginal Elders helped Ruby and me understand our culture and told us what our Dreaming spirits were. Mine is a wedge-tailed eagle and Ruby's is a pelican.

This book was the last project Ruby and I worked on together.
Ruby passed away in 2010, before the first picture book was published. Her Dreaming spirit, the Pelican, returned to the Milky Way, that mighty river of stars in the sky, where she remains to this day. When I look at the night sky there is always one star that seems to twinkle brighter than the rest and I know that's her!

People like me, we think in circles. We make a journey in life, and life being a circle, we follow that circle. If that circle gets broken, people don't know what to do, they become confused. But there's a good way we can join that circle back up again and that's by reaching out. Joining hands. The circle's healed. Linked up, all the people, together again.

The Archie Roach Foundation logo represents my mother's spirit animal, the wedge-tailed eagle, and my father's spirit animal, the red-bellied black snake. It's also about me coming full circle, back to who I was taken from. I didn't know my mother and father, but I have stories about them. That's why we have stories to let us know who we are and where we are from, to join us up, connect us, to complete the circle.

Took the Children Away

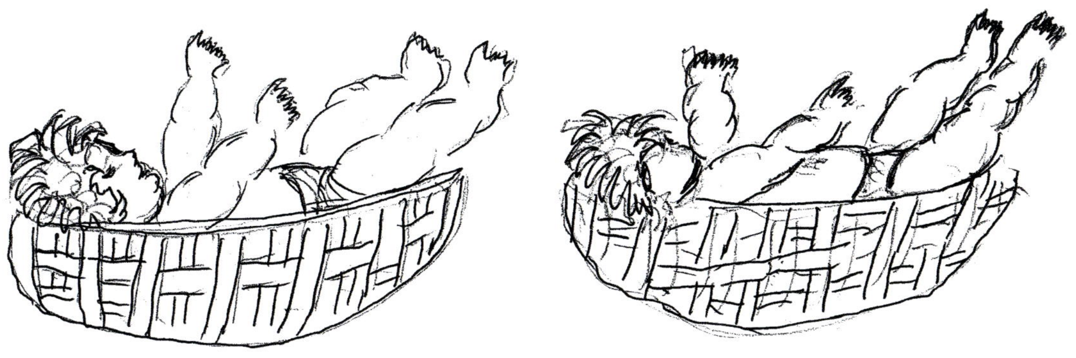

Archie Roach

with illustrations by Ruby Hunter

SIMON & SCHUSTER

London · New York · Sydney · Toronto · New Delhi

This is an old photo of me and my Uncle Banjo Clarke walking through the forest near Framlingham Aboriginal Mission, the place where I was taken from. Uncle Banjo was an Elder who told stories that connected me to my mother Nellie Austin and my Gunditjmara family in southwest Victoria.

Uncle Banjo heard I was writing songs and asked me to write a song about when I was taken away. I told him that I was only two years old and so did not remember. He looked at me and said, 'Yeah, but I do.' He then told me the story about when I was taken that dark day on Framlingham. I thought, this isn't just about us being taken away, it's also about who we were taken from. So I wrote the song 'Took the Children Away'.

This story's right this story's true
I would not tell lies to you
Like the promises they did not keep
And how they fenced us in like sheep

Said to us come take our hand
Sent us off on mission land
Taught us to read to write and pray
Then they took the children away
Took the children away
The children away
Snatched from their mother's breast
Said it was for the best
Took them away

The welfare and the policeman
Said you've got to understand
We'll give to them what you can't give
Teach them how to really live

THE WELFare
THE POLICEMAN
POLICE
POLICE
Foster Care and AdopTion Care
JaiLs and INSTITUTIONS

Took
The
children
Away
History
LESSON
THIS STORIES
RIGHT
THIS STORIES
TRUE

Teach them how to live they said
Humiliated them instead
Taught them that and taught them this
And others taught them prejudice

You took the children away
The children away
Breaking their mother's heart
Tearing us all apart
Took them away

One dark day on Framlingham
Came and didn't give a damn
My mother cried go get their dad
He came running fighting mad

Mother's tears were falling down
Dad shaped up and stood his ground
He said 'You touch my kids and you fight me'
And they took us from our family
Took them away

Took us away
They took us away
Snatched from our mother's breast
Said this was for the best
Took us away

Told us what to do and say
Told us all the white man's ways
Then they split us up again
And gave us gifts to ease the pain

Sent us off to foster homes
As we grew up we felt alone
'Cause we were acting white
Yet feeling black

One sweet day all the children came back
The children came back
The children came back
Back where their hearts grow strong
Back where they all belong

The children came back
Said the children came back
The children came back
Back where they understand
Back to their mother's land
The children came back

Back to their mother
Back to their father
Back to their sister
Back to their brother
Back to their people
Back to their land

All the children came back
The children came back
The children came back
Yes I came back

This is the only photo, taken in 1940, that I have of my mother and father, Nellie Austin and Archie Roach, with their first baby – my eldest brother Johnny Roach – later in life affectionately nicknamed Horse.

I was taken from my family at the age of two, along with two of my sisters, Gladys and Diana, and sent to the Salvation Army Girls' Home in East Camberwell, also known as the William Booth Orphanage.

This is one of the only photos I have of me as a child, taken in 1961 when I was five years old.

This is my father, Archie Roach, outside our home on Framlingham Aboriginal Mission, with my big sister Myrtle peeking around him at the photographer.

Here are photos of my sisters Diana and Gladys. At the time these photos were taken, Gladys (left) was in Grade 3 at Canterbury State School and Diana (right) was in Form 1 at Canterbury Girls' College.

This photo of me as the Form 2D class captain at Lilydale High School, taken in 1969, came from my ward file. It had been in my ward file for fifty years.

Me and my brothers, somewhere in Fitzroy, late '70s (from left): Johnny 'Horse', me, our friend Darren and Lawrence. This is the only photo I have of me and my brothers.

My sisters Alma (left) and Myrtle with Ruby (centre) about to board the bus from Melbourne to Sydney for the 1988 Bicentenary Protest.

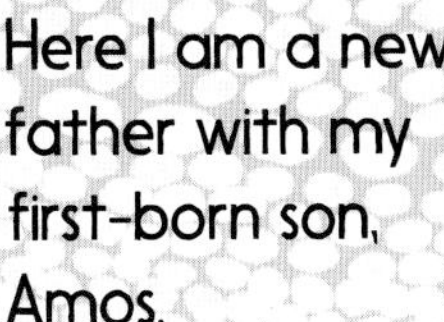

Here I am a new father with my first-born son, Amos.

This is a photo of our home life taken for *Who* magazine, 14 February 1992. The caption read: 'At home, Roach gets his kicks from family life with (from left) Eban, 12, Amos, 13, Arthur, 14, Terrence, 3, and Ruby'.

Ruby grew up on the sand dunes and saltwater lagoons of the Coorong in South Australia with her grandmother, Nan Tingie, and her sister and brothers.

One day, when Ruby was a little girl, the welfare came and told Nan Tingie they were taking the children to the circus and would bring them back later. But Nan Tingie never saw the children again.

This is a rare photo of Ruby as a little girl.

After Ruby was taken from Nan Tingie, she was separated again from her sister and brothers and grew up in a foster home. Like me, Ruby eventually found her sister and brothers and went on to write and sing songs about her own life.

Ruby was a proud Ngarrindjeri, Kokatha, Pitjantjatjara woman. The one thing she was most proud of was keeping her family together. This photo shows Ruby, me and the boys at our home in Clingin Street in Reservoir in the early '90s.

The painting opposite is by Ruby's sister-in-law, Rosslyn Richards, and is titled 'NO:RI has landed'. NO:RI is a Ngarrindjeri word meaning Pelican. When home from touring, Ruby would contact family to let them know she had arrived safely and would say 'the NO:RI has landed'.

RR

When I wrote the song 'Took the Children Away', I never imagined that people from other countries would relate to this song. I did not realise that other children around the world had been taken away from their families as well.

In Canada someone told me that many, many First Nations children there were taken away from their families and sent to residential schools. So it's not just my story or Ruby's story – it's their story too. They said that my song had become a healing song. I can understand that, because every time I sing this song I let a little bit of the pain go, and I have been singing it for a long time now. One day, maybe soon, through the healing power of music, I will let it all go.

To listen to Archie singing 'Took the Children Away', and to discover more archival photos and stories about Archie and Ruby, go to www.archieroach.com/charcoallane

Special thanks to Jill Shelton, Clare Forster and Alexis Steere

Image credits

Lake Condah possum-skin cloak design © Gunditj Mirring Traditional Owners Aboriginal Corporation RNTBC. This artwork on the front and back cover previously appeared on Archie Roach's 2007 *Journey* album and is reproduced here with kind permission from the Gunditj Mirring Traditional Owners.

Introduction – Photograph of Ruby and Archie at Sing Sing Studios Richmond in 1996 by Tim Webster (www.timwebster.com.au), reproduced with kind permission.

p 1,4 – Artwork by Alexis Steere, from the *Tell Me Why* deluxe CD edition 2019, reproduced with kind permission.

pp 2, 28–30 – Artwork by Kurun Warun (kurunwarun.com), reproduced with kind permission.

p 4 – Photograph of Uncle Banjo Clarke and Archie walking through the Framlingham Forest in 1990 is a still from the 1991 episode 'Best Kept Secret' from the ABC program *Blackout*. Reproduced by permission of the Australian Broadcasting Corporation – Library Sales © 1991 ABC.

p 5 – Artwork from the *Into the Bloodstream* album cover (2012) featuring a painting of Framlingham Aboriginal Mission by Rob Lowe Senior, reproduced with kind permission.

pp 6–26 – Artwork by Tracy Roach in the background of the pages containing the lyrics of 'Took the Children Away' reproduced with kind permission.

p 24 – Photograph by Pierre Baroni, reproduced with kind permission.

p 27 – Photograph by Mike Bowers from a 19 January 1993 *Age* article on Aboriginal identity, reproduced with kind permission.

p 28–30 – Archival photos provided with kind permission from the Roach and Hunter families.

P 30 – Photograph of Ruby performing by Wendell Teodoro, from the Murundak show on January 22nd 2008 at the Sydney Opera House as part of the Sydney Festival, reproduced with kind permission.

p 31 – 'NO:RI has landed', painted by Rosslyn Richards, reproduced with kind permission.

p 32 – Photograph by Maree Clarke, 1990, reproduced with kind permission.

TOOK THE CHILDREN AWAY

First published in Australia in 2020 by
Simon & Schuster (Australia) Pty Limited
Level 4, 32 York Street
Sydney, NSW 2000

10 9 8 7 6 5 4

Sydney New York London Toronto New Delhi
Visit our website at www.simonandschuster.com.au

A previous picture book featuring Archie's lyrics and some of Ruby's artwork was published by One Day Hill in 2010.

A catalogue record for this book is available from the National Library of Australia

Publishing project management: Erica Wagner
Additional artwork and assistance: Craig Smith
Cover and text design: Joanna Hunt
Typesetting: Joanna Hunt

Printed and bound in China by Leo Paper Products